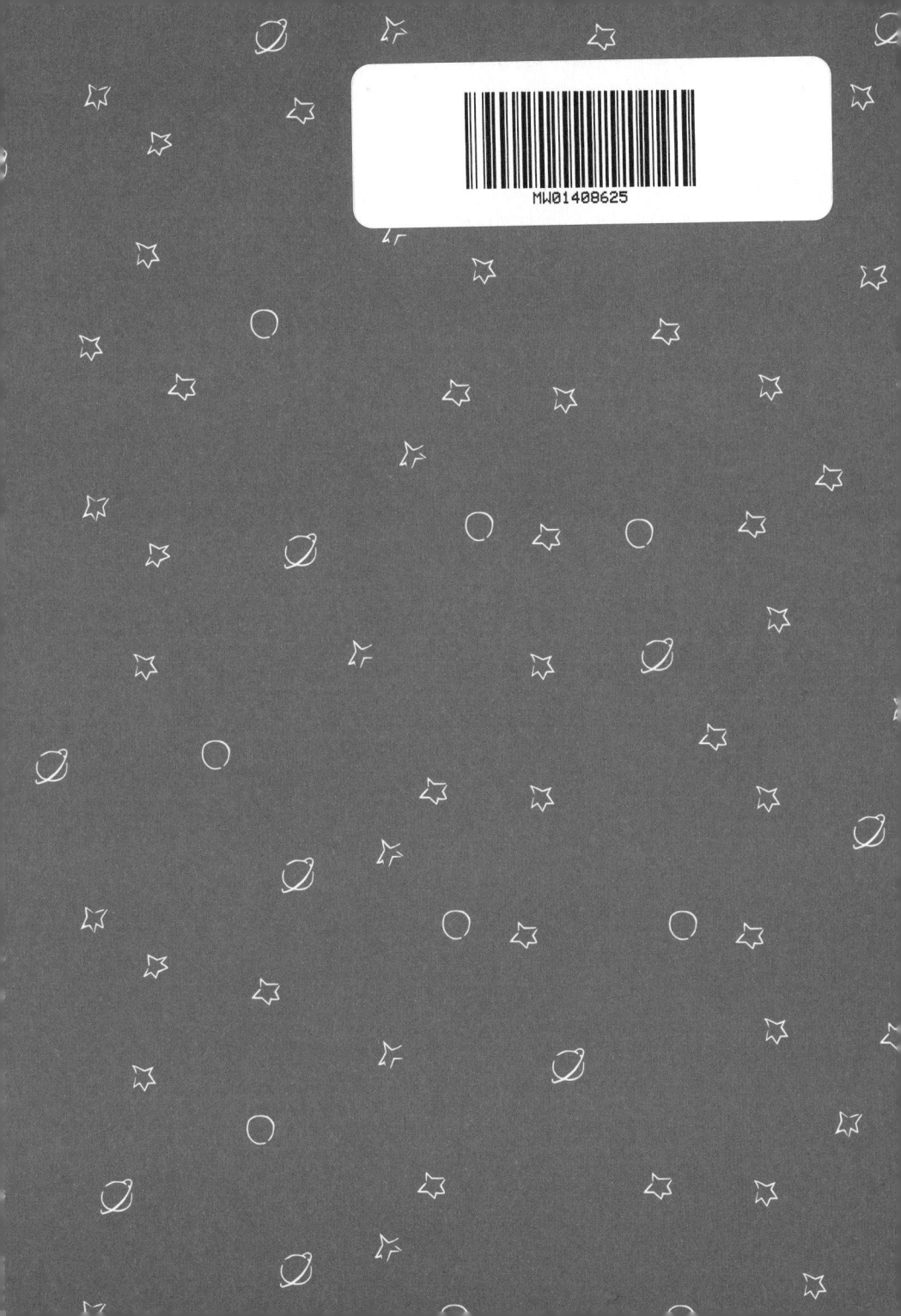

The Little Prince

a journal

RP STUDIO

> Words have power. They bind us, remind us, and connect us to the world. No book will ever be as powerful as the one that you write for your own child. So record the exquisite, explosive joy of the first latch, the first smile, the first laugh, the first step, the first word. It is a story that is completely original.
>
> All my love,
> Katherine

The Little Prince™/Le Petit Prince®
©Antoine de Saint-Exupéry Estate 2018

Hachette Book Group supports the right to free expression and the value of copyright. The purpose of copyright is to encourage writers and artists to produce the creative works that enrich our culture.

The scanning, uploading, and distribution of this book without permission is a theft of the author's intellectual property. If you would like permission to use material from the book (other than for review purposes), please contact permissions@hbgusa.com. Thank you for your support of the author's rights.

RP Studio
Hachette Book Group
1290 Avenue of the Americas,
New York, NY 10104
www.runningpress.com
@Running_Press

Printed in China
First Edition: October 2018

Published by RP Studio, an imprint of Perseus Books, LLC, a subsidiary of Hachette Book Group, Inc. The RP Studio name and logo is a trademark of the Hachette Book Group.

The publisher is not responsible for websites (or their content) that are not owned by the publisher.

Designed by Jenna McBride.

ISBN: 978-0-7624-6501-9 (hardcover)

L-REX

10 9 8 7 6 5 4 3 2 1

"We write of eternal things..."

"All grown-ups were children first."

"(But few of them remember it.)"

"The thing
that is
important

is

the thing

that is

not seen."

☆

"The proof that the little prince
existed is that he was charming,
that he laughed, and that
he was looking for a sheep.

If anybody wants a sheep,
that is a proof that he exists."

☆

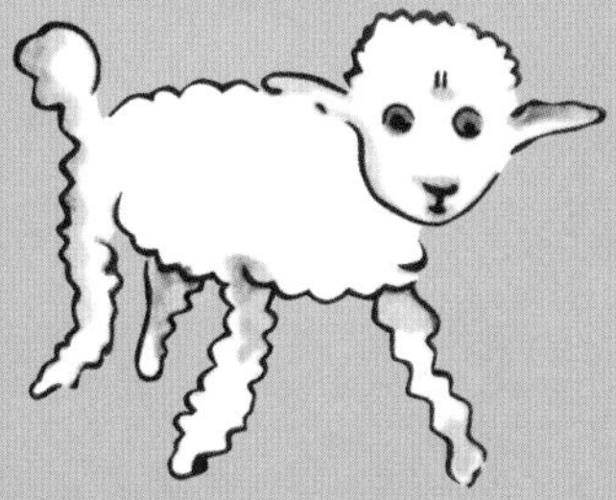

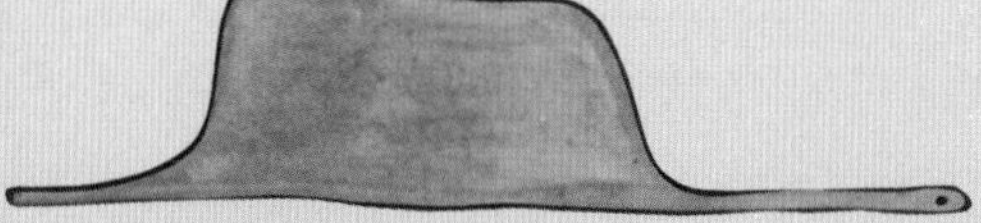

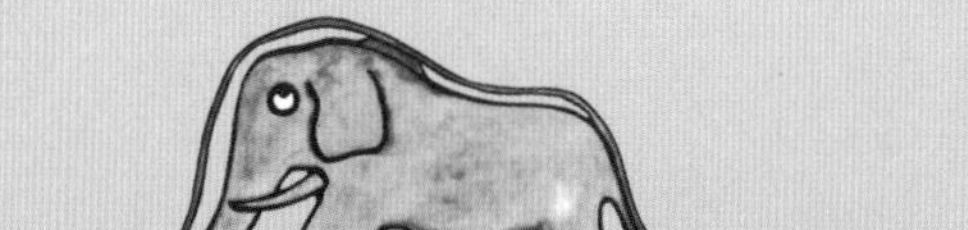

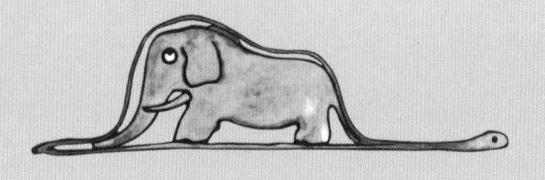

"My drawing was not a picture of a hat. It was a picture of a boa constrictor digesting an elephant."

"There is no harm in

putting off

a piece of work

until

another day."

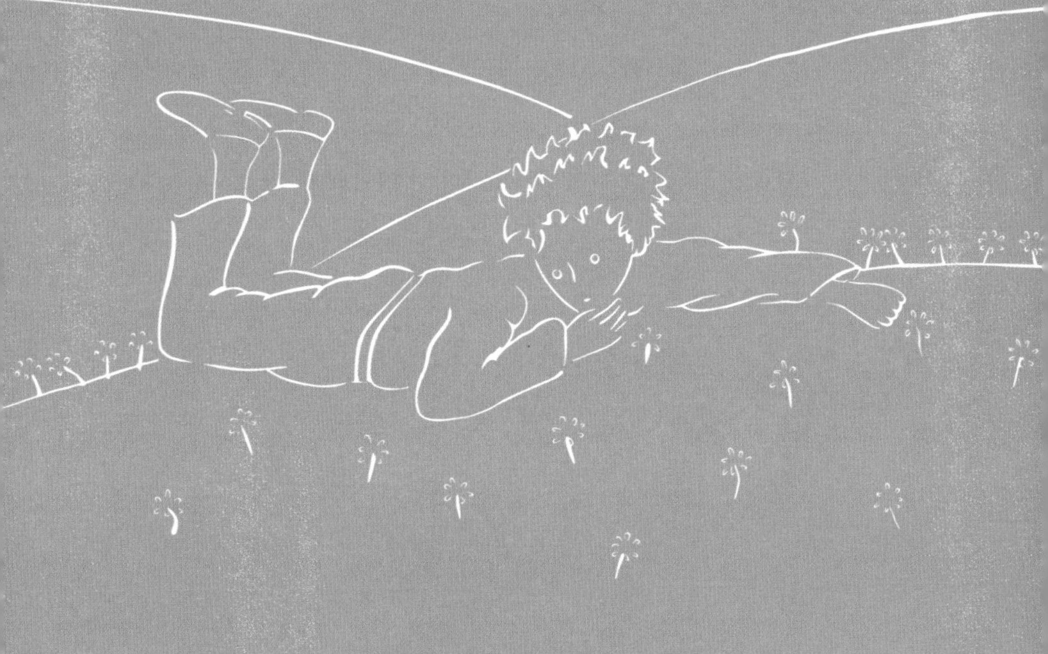

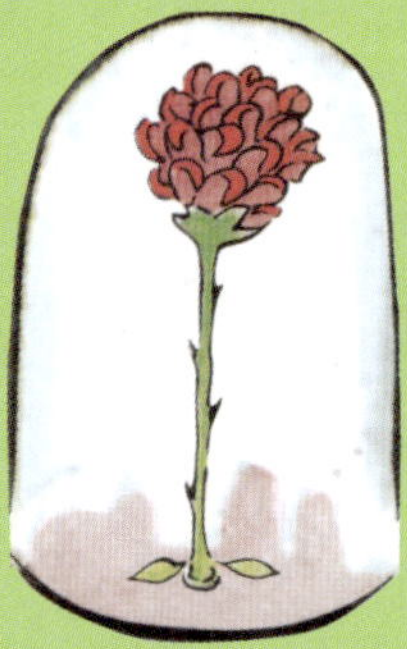

☆

"You become responsible,
forever, for what you have tamed.
You are responsible for your rose."

☆

"I like my

misfortunes

to be taken

seriously."

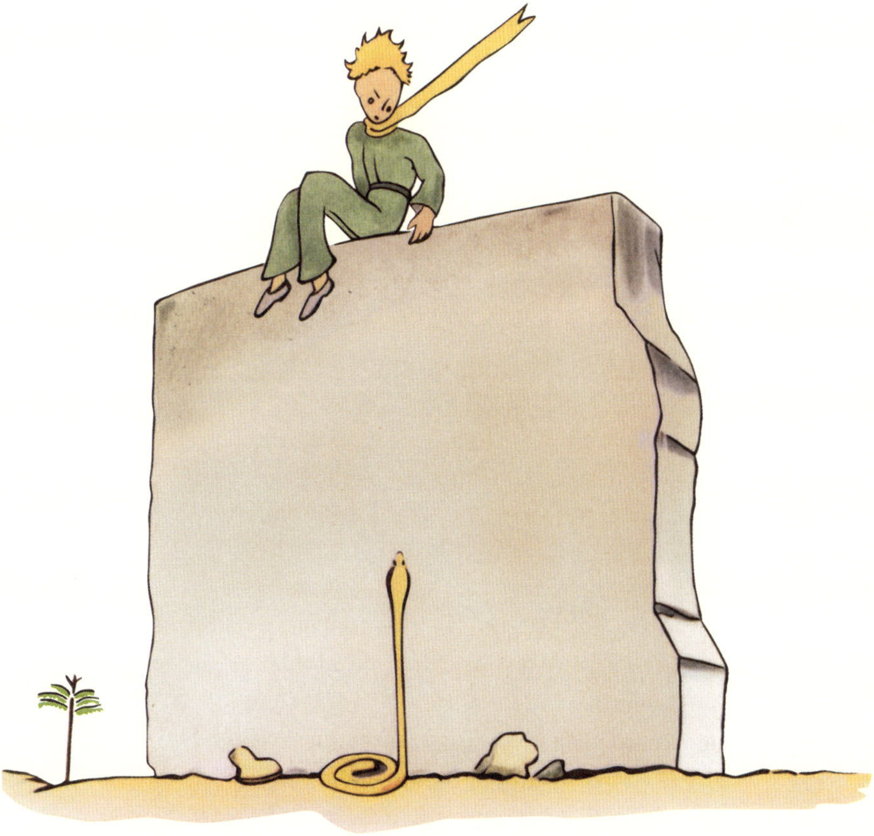

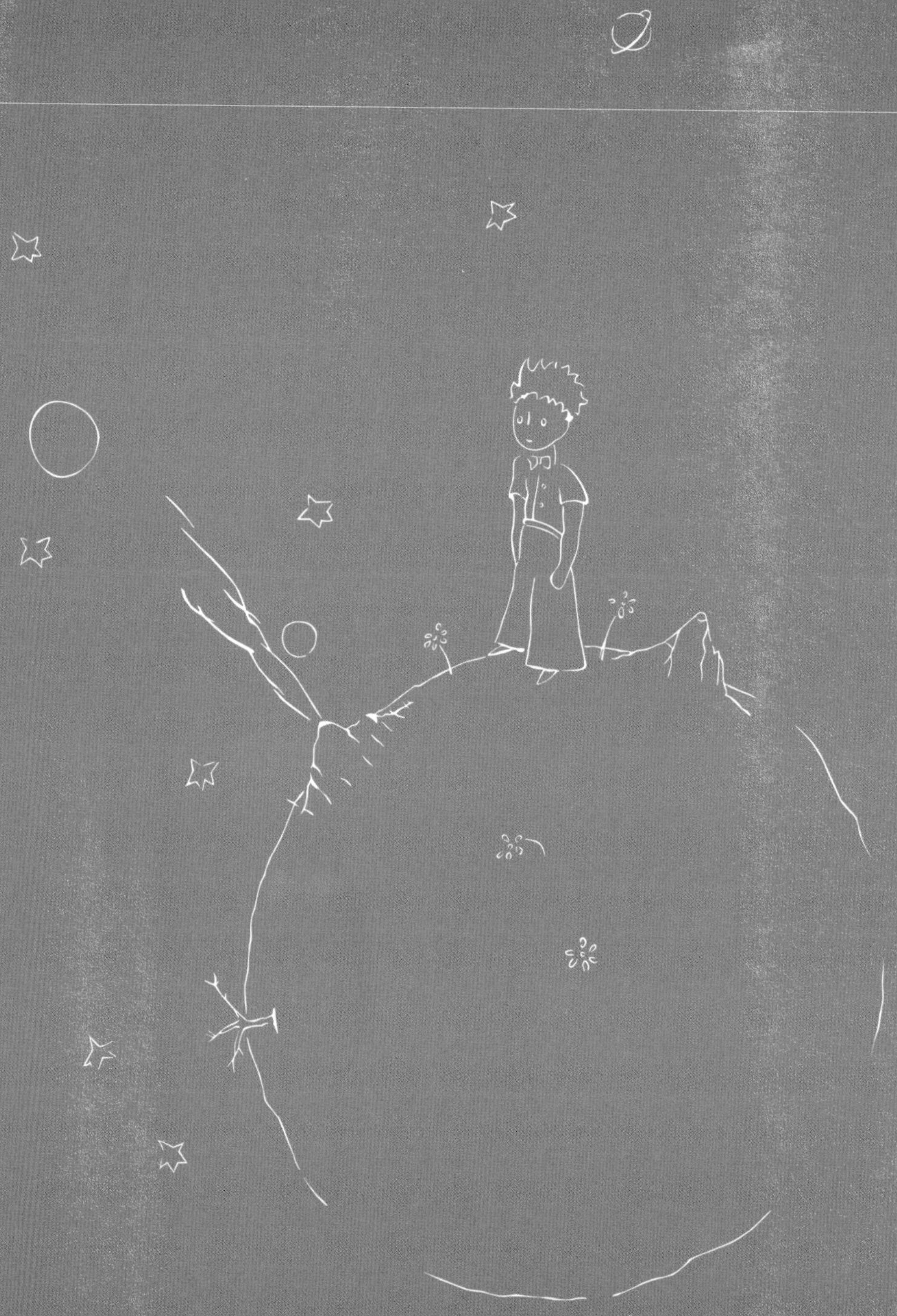

☆

"I have serious reason to believe
that the planet from which the
little prince came is the
asteroid known as B-612."

☆

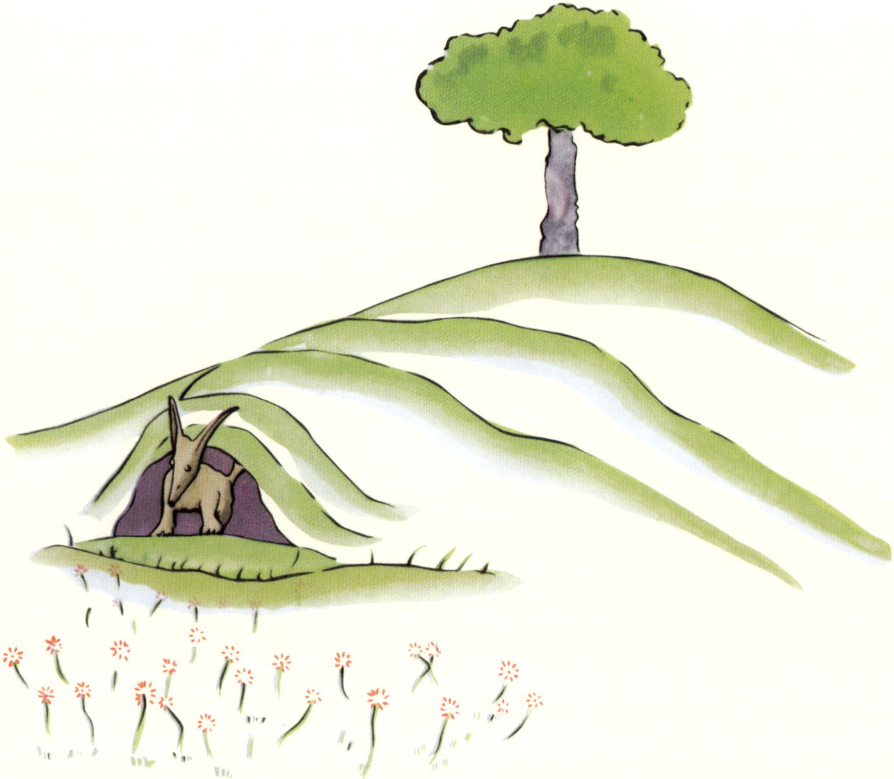

"Children should always show great **forbearance** toward grown-up people."

"To forget a friend is sad.

Not
every one
has had a
friend."

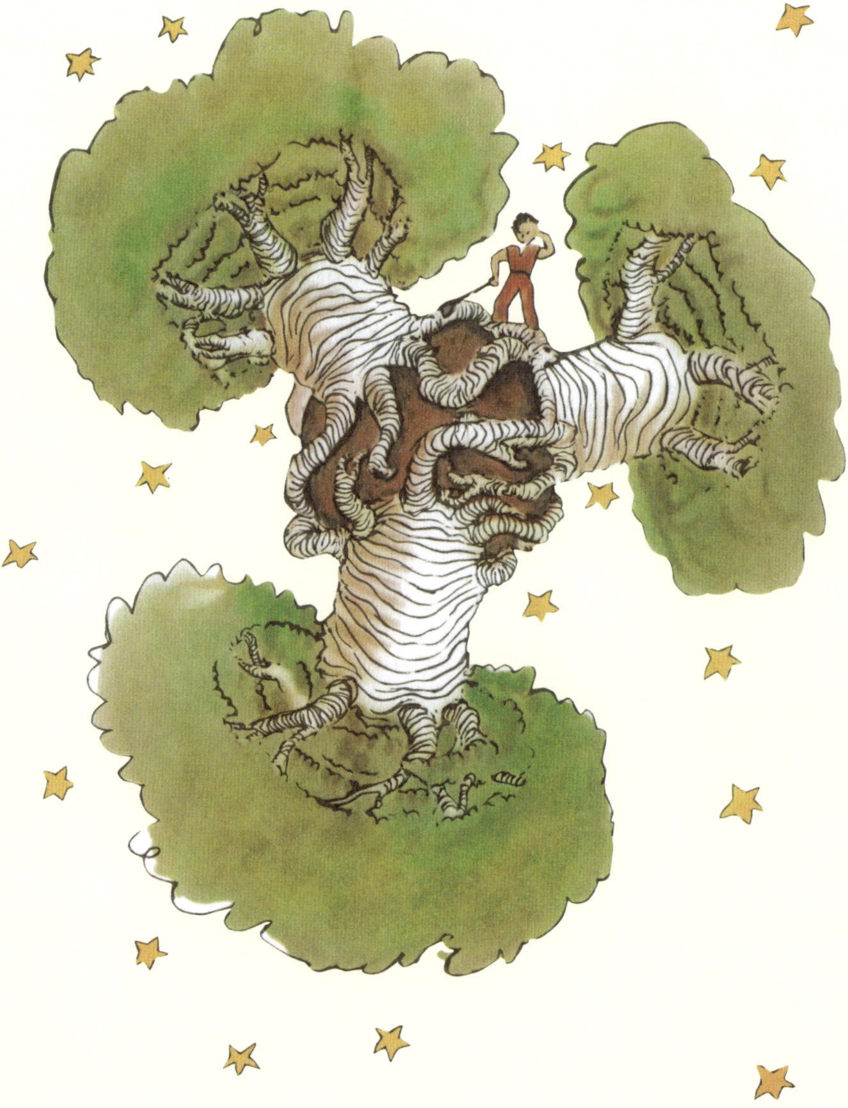

"A baobab is something you will never, never be able to get rid of if you attend to it too late."

☆

"His flower had told him that she was the only one of her kind in all the universe. And here were five thousand of them, all alike, in one single garden!"

☆

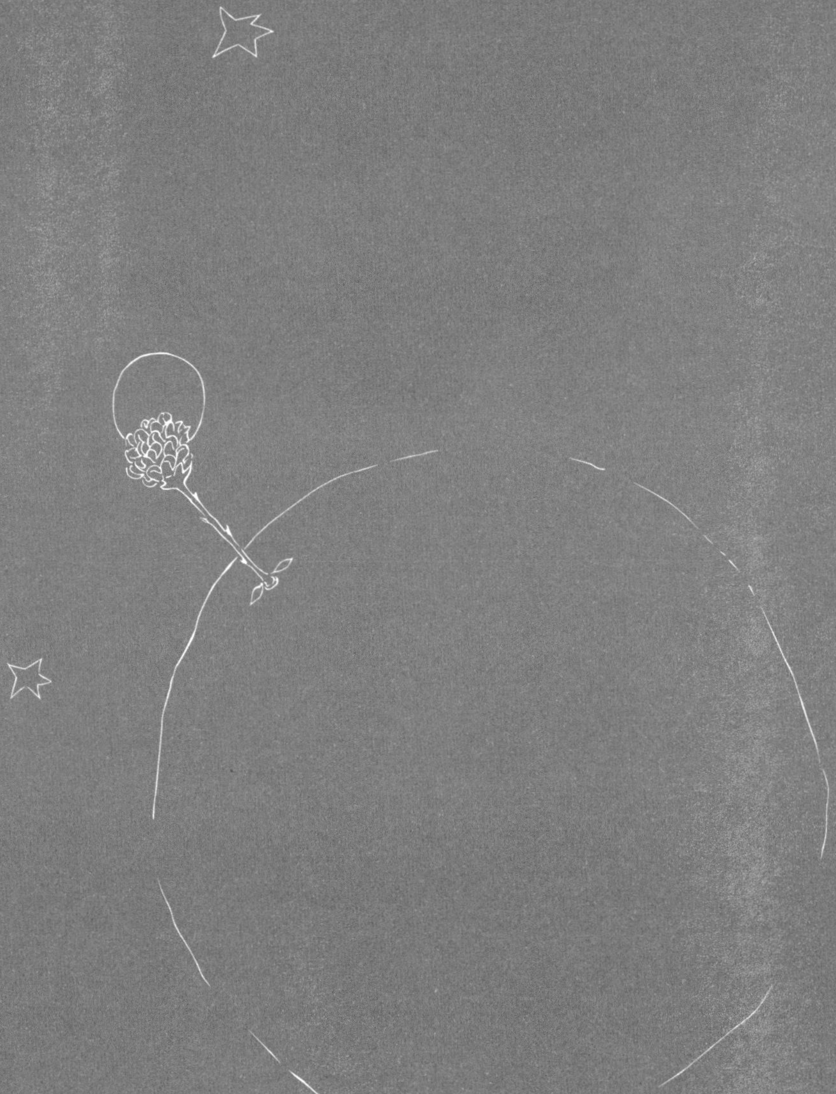

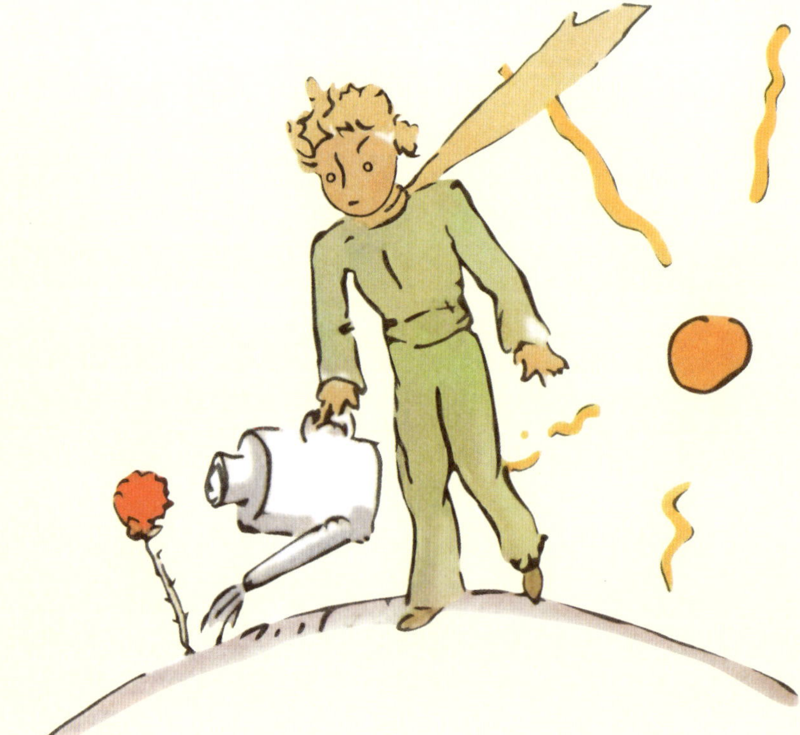

☆

"But in herself alone she is more important than all the hundreds of you other roses: because it is she that I have watered."

☆

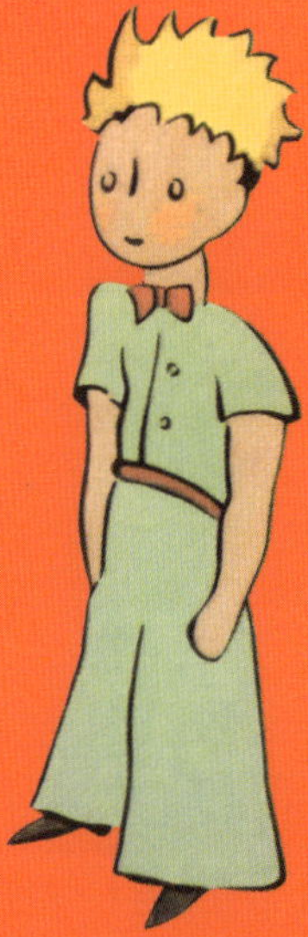

"Words are the source of misunderstandings."

"It is the time

you have wasted

for your rose

that makes your rose so

important."

"When you've **finished** your own toilet in the **morning,** then it is time to attend

to the toilet of

your planet,

just so, with the

greatest care."

"My home
was hiding a secret

in the depths of its

heart…"

"It is such a
secret place,
the
land of tears."

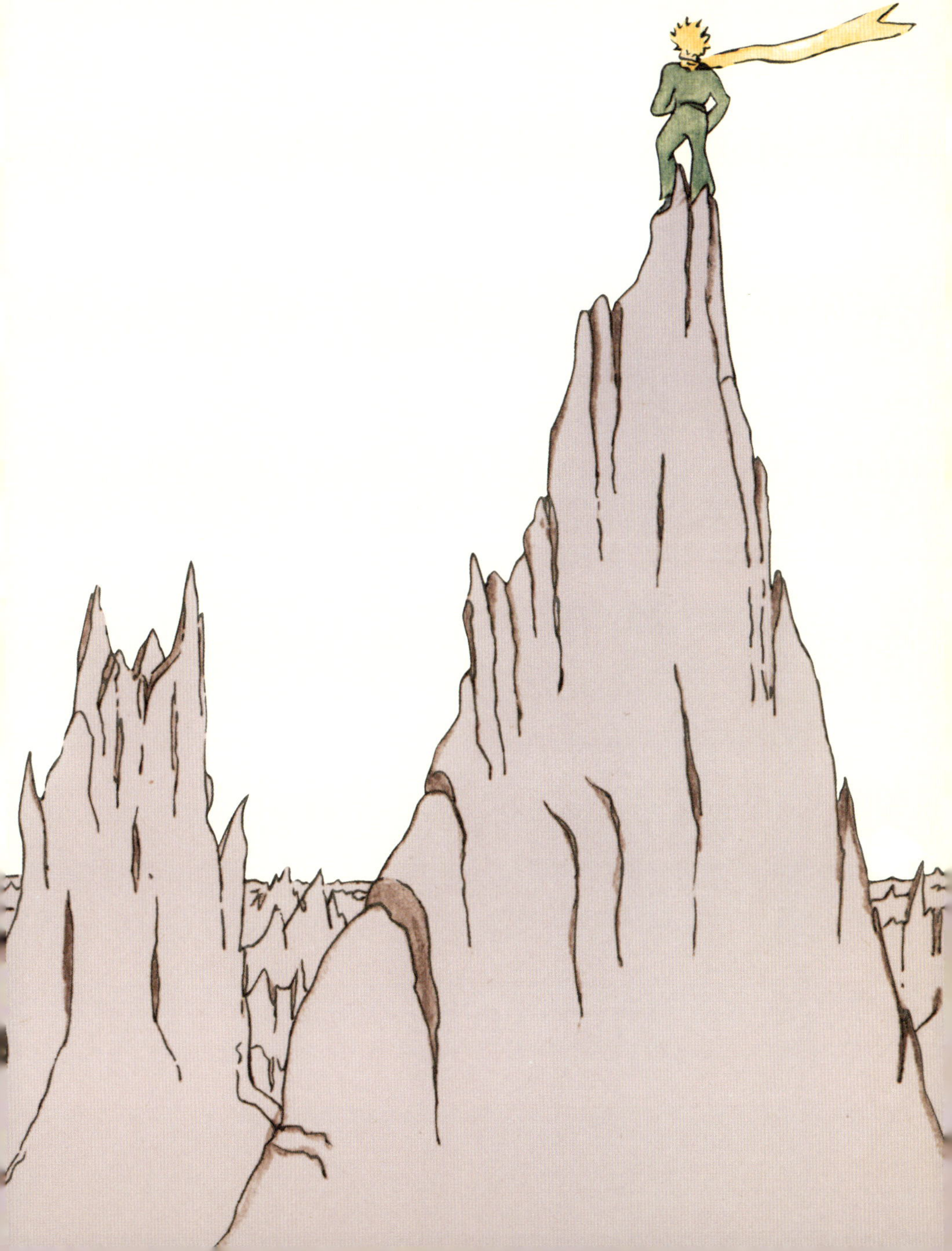

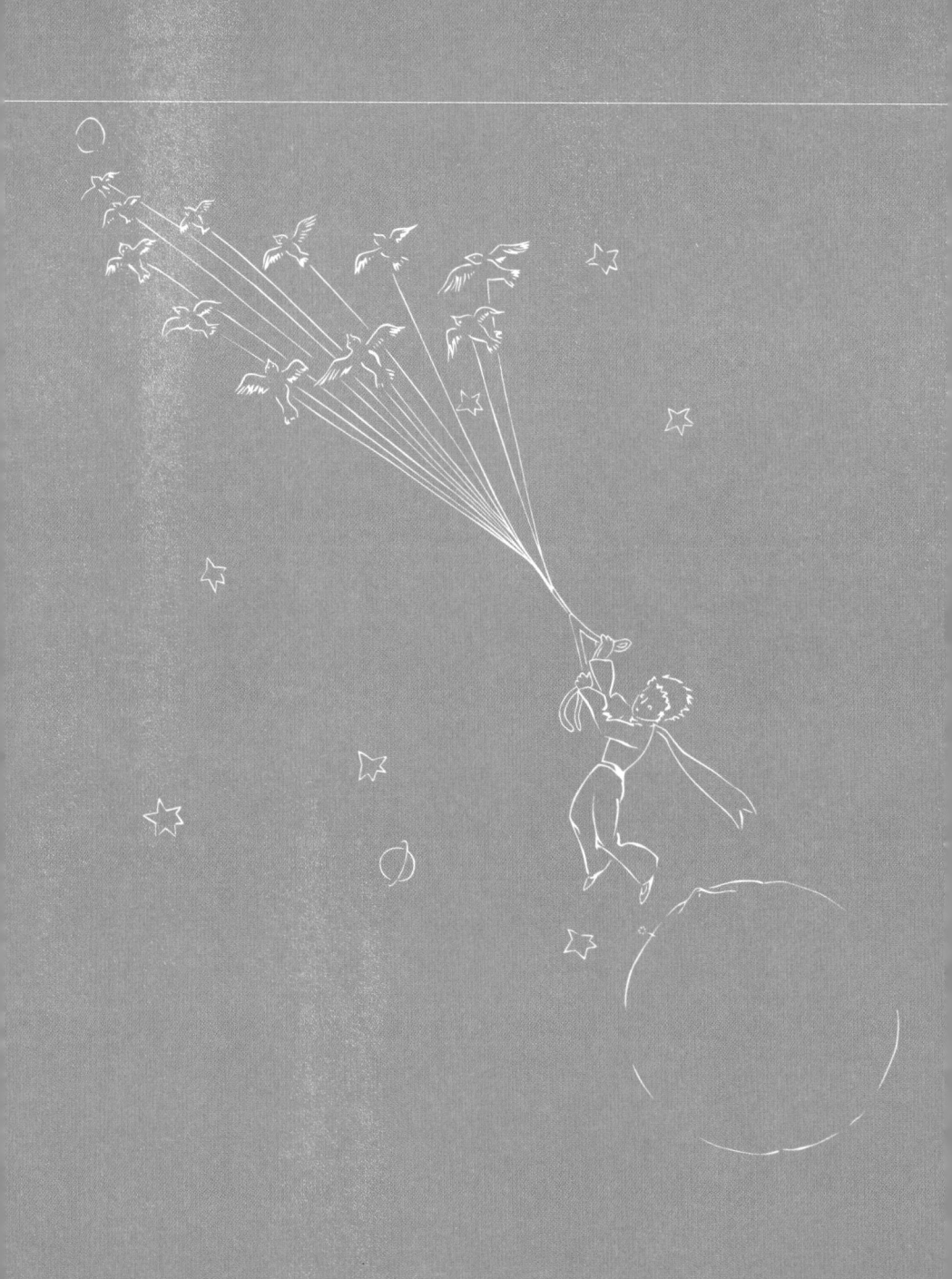

☆

"If some one loves a flower, of which just one single blossom grows in all the millions and millions of stars, it is enough to make him happy just to look at the stars."

☆

"It is much more difficult to **judge oneself** than to judge others."

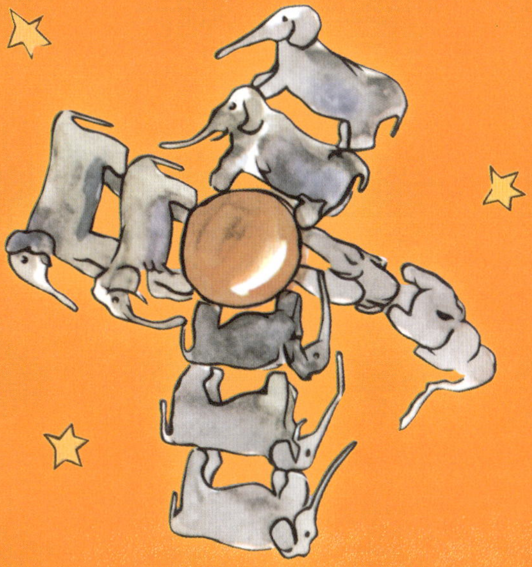

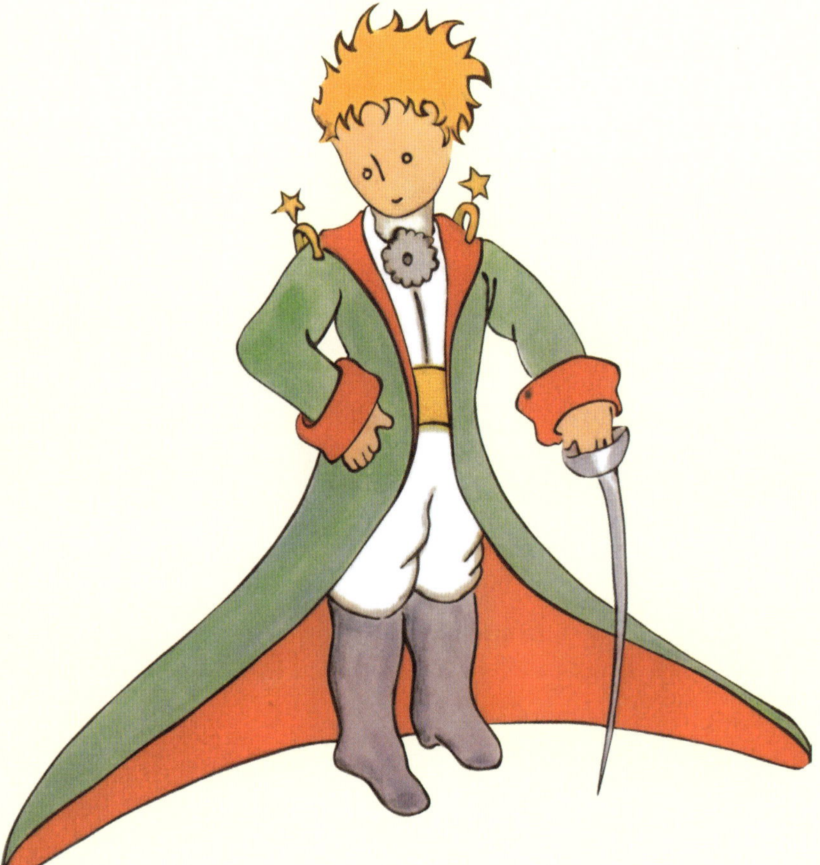

"If you succeed in
judging yourself
rightly,
then you are indeed a man of
true wisdom."

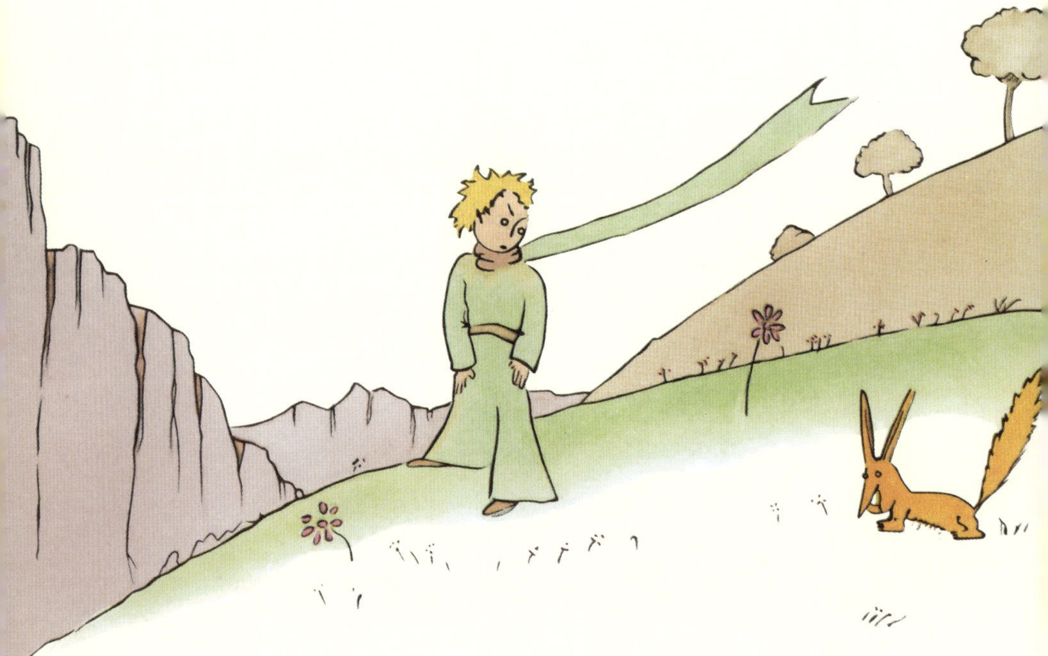

☆

"To you, I am nothing more than a fox like a hundred thousand other foxes. But if you tame me, then we shall need each other. To me, you will be unique in all the world. To you, I shall be unique in all the world."

☆

"There is a flower...
I think that she has tamed me."

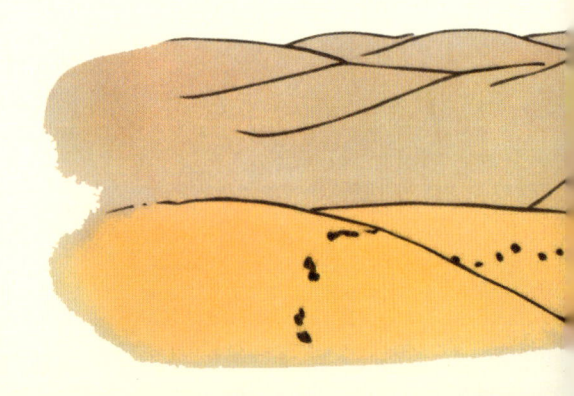

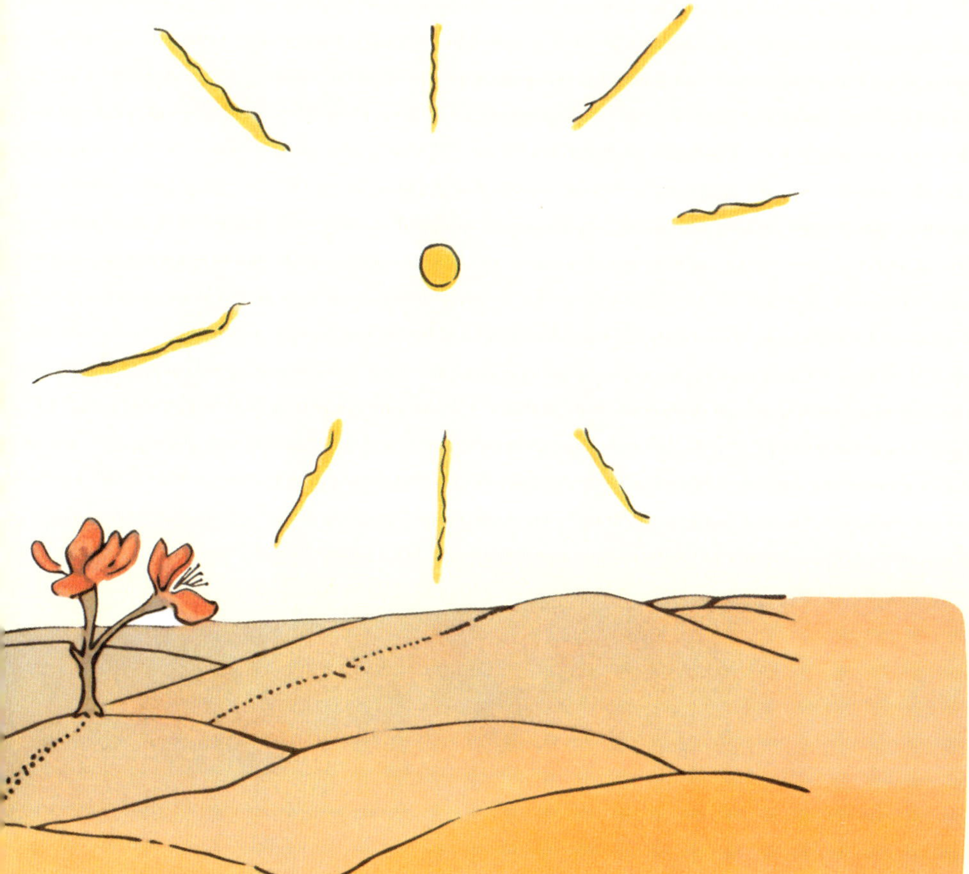

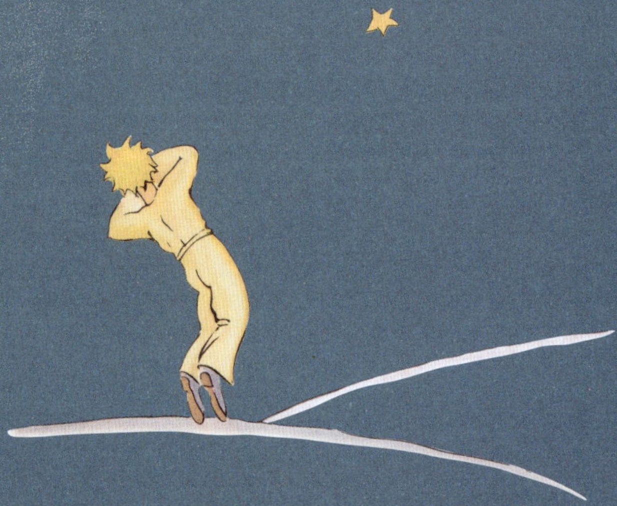

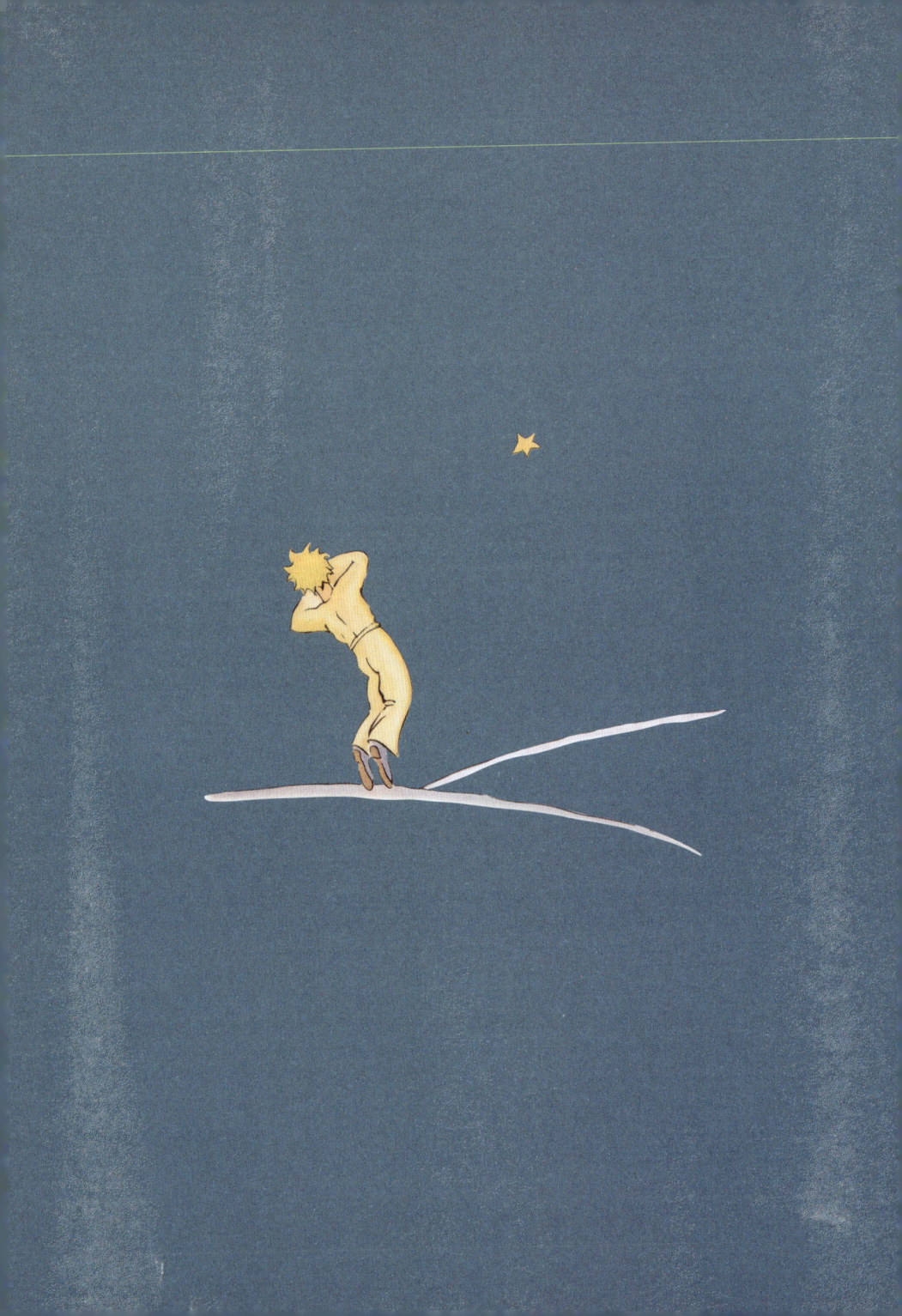

"What moves me so deeply, about this
little prince who is sleeping here,
is his loyalty to a flower—the image
of a rose that shines through his
whole being like the flame of a lamp,
even when he is asleep."

"But the eyes are blind. One must look with the heart."

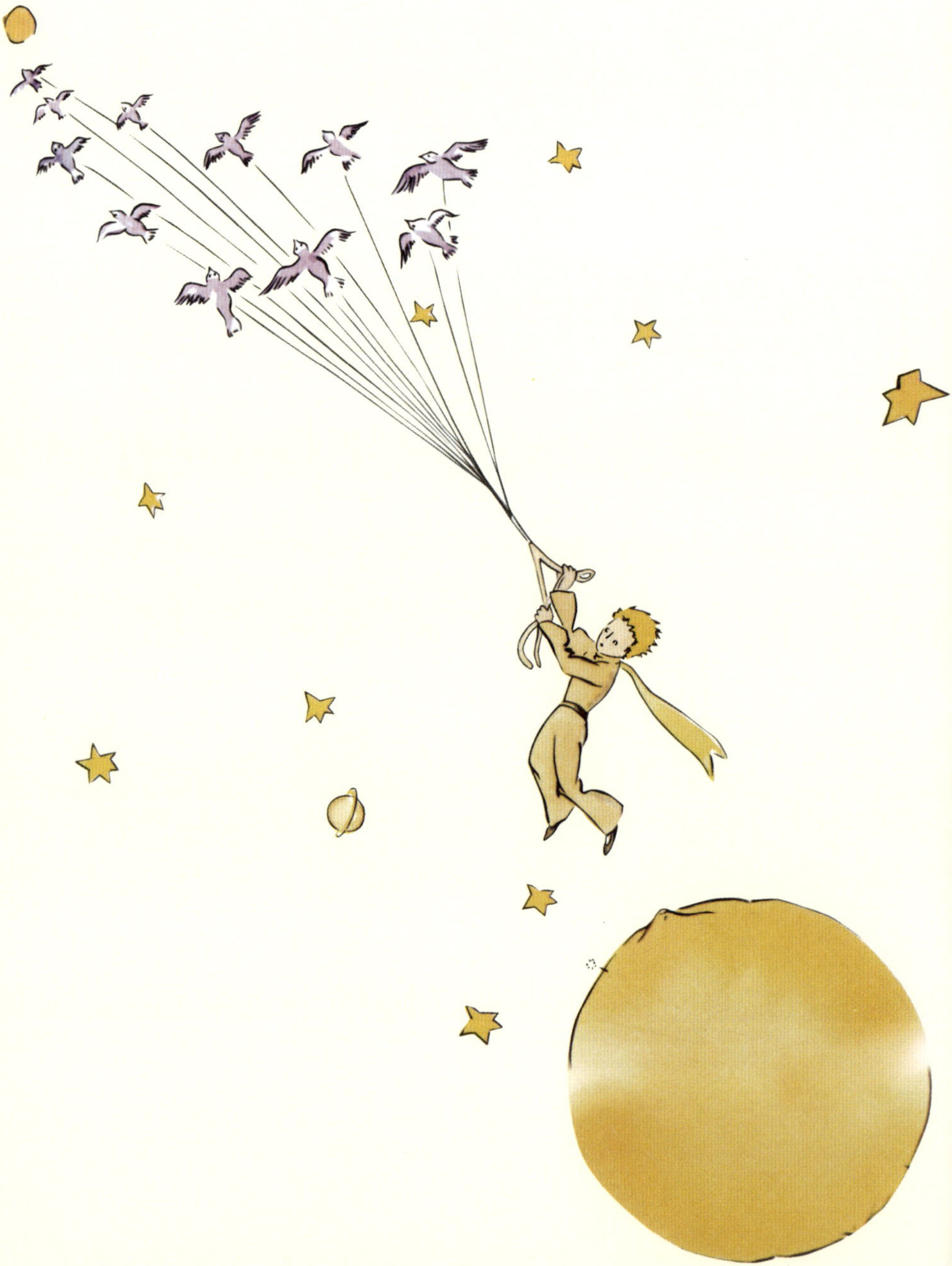

"For some,

who are travelers,

the stars

are guides."

☆

"In one of the stars I shall be living.
In one of them I shall be laughing.
And so it will be as if all the stars were
laughing, when you look at the sky
at night…you, only you, will have
stars that can laugh!"

☆

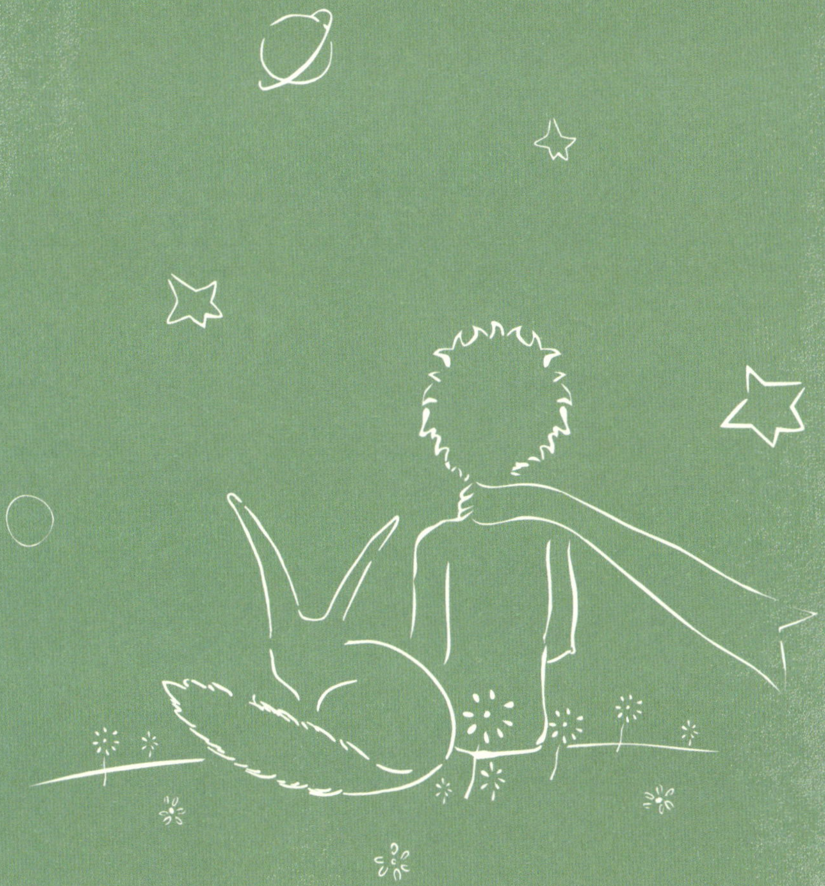

"And now here is
my secret,
a very **simple** secret:

It is only with the heart that one can see rightly; what is essential is invisible to the eye."

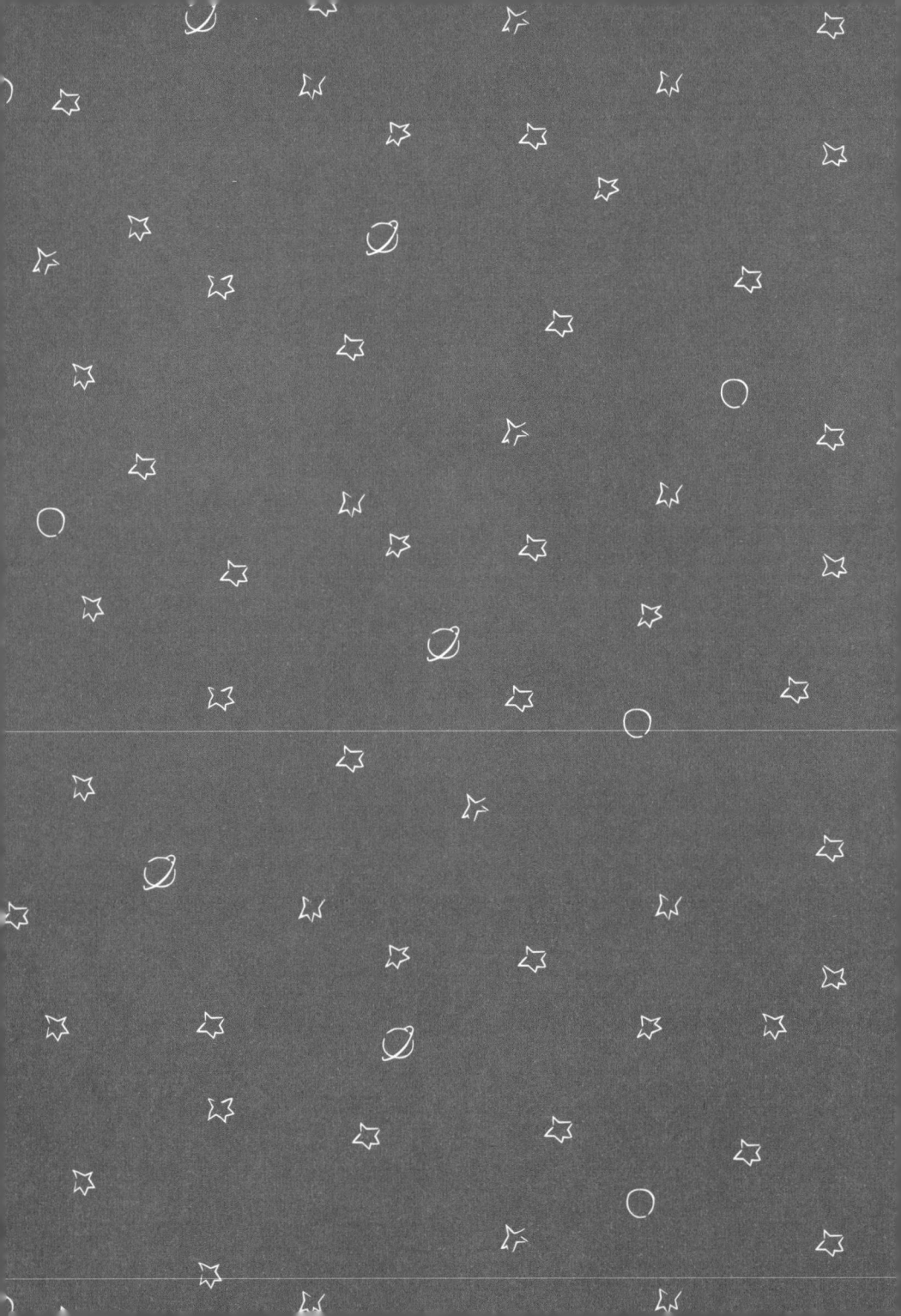